GOOD DOG!

Sean Taylor
& David Barrow

Frances Lincoln
Children's Books

I have all sorts of **brilliant** fun with my owner. He's called Melvin.

Sometimes he likes me **so much,**

he smiles and says,

"GOOD DOG!"

GOOD DOG!

Para os meus sogros queridos,
Anna Carolina e Walter – ST

For Matt and Emma – DB

Brimming with creative inspiration, how-to projects, and useful information to enrich your everyday life, Quarto Knows is a favourite destination for those pursuing their interests and passions. Visit our site and dig deeper with our books into your area of interest: Quarto Creates, Quarto Cooks, Quarto Homes, Quarto Lives, Quarto Drives, Quarto Explores, Quarto Gifts, or Quarto Kids.

Inspiring | Educating | Creating | Entertaining

Good Dog! © 2020 Quarto Publishing plc.
Text © 2020 Sean Taylor. Illustrations © 2020 David Barrow.
First published in 2020 by Frances Lincoln Children's Books,
an imprint of The Quarto Group.
First published in paperback in 2020 by Frances Lincoln Children's Books.
The Old Brewery, 6 Blundell Street, London N7 9BH, United Kingdom.
T (0)20 7700 6700 F (0)20 7700 8066 www.QuartoKnows.com

A catalogue record for this book is available from the British Library.
ISBN 978-1-78603-726-8
The illustrations were created with graphite and coloured pencil.
Set in Roboto Slab.
Published by Katie Cotton. Designed by Zoë Tucker
Edited by Katy Flint. Production by Nicolas Zeifman and Caragh McAleenan.
Manufactured in Guangdong, China EB042020

1 3 5 7 9 8 6 4 2

That makes me feel
woo-hoo,
all over!

But yesterday, Melvin left an
extra-delicious-smelling pizza
on the table.

When he came back,
one small slice was missing.

I gazed at him, in a very loving
sort of way. I tried my best to
look like it was nothing to
do with me.

That wasn't likely to work,
when there was cheese on
my chin and tomato
in my ear.

But it was still a sad moment for me,
when Melvin pointed and said...

"BAD DOG!"

Bad? Me??

I felt completely full of unhappy feelings. So I promised myself I would definitely make Melvin smile again and say, 'Good Dog!'

I had a fantastic plan for this.
Sometimes, when Melvin lies
down to relax,

I jump on him, and I give him
a surprise sniffle-snuggle!
That usually makes him smile and say,

"GOOD
DOG!"

So, the next time
he was lying down, I got ready for
a special surprise sniffle-snuggle...

Then I jumped on him.

But I think I chose a bad time.
Melvin didn't smile.
And he didn't say

"GOOD
DOG!"

It was a difficult night.

I felt **boo-hoo**, all over!
But I said to myself, "Tomorrow
is **always** another day..."

And, when Melvin came down in the morning, I had a very genius idea! He was in a hurry to go to work. So I **helped him get dressed fast.**

I fetched him socks,

then trousers.

And also pants...

Melvin liked that. He smiled!
And all my instincts told me
he was going to say,

"GOOD DOG!"

I was filled with such a
happy-dog feeling that I did a
whopping wag
of my tail!

And I tipped
over a stool,

which pushed over
Melvin's bicycle,

which knocked
a telephone off
the table

and smashed
a lamp into
bits.

DOG SHOW

Melvin
stopped smiling.
He didn't say
"GOOD DOG!"

He picked up the broken bits.

He looked at his watch and
grabbed a sandwich. Then he
slammed the fridge door
and went to work.

I was as sad as one lonely tear
all on its own...

until I noticed something.
A packet of sausages had fallen out of the fridge!

Straight away, I made a
plan that would put me
back in a good mood.

First this.

Then this.

Then
yummy!
Yum, yum, yum!

But I had a new thought.

If I left the sausages alone, Melvin would be
pleased with me! I found myself with one of those
life-changing choices we sometimes get.
And I decided . . .

I would NOT eat the sausages!

This put me in a completely difficult situation. I told my eyes to stay shut tight, so I couldn't see the sausages. But one of them kept on opening up!

I went to sleep.
But I had a dream about sausages dancing at a party for sausages.

Even so, I did **not** touch the sausages.

And when Melvin came back,
he smiled. Then he said,

"GOOD DOG!"

It made me feel
whoopy doopy doo,
all over!

I was so pleased, I wanted to
do the **jumping jive,**

the **twist**

and the
hippy-hippy shake,
with my tail!

But I remembered what had happened before.

So I kept my tail **completely** under control.
And everything was fine except...

I was **SO** excited . . .

I did a bit of a wee-wee on the floor.

I looked at Melvin, to see what he thought.
His eyes were closed. And I said to myself,
"Tomorrow is **always** another day..."

Also by Sean Taylor and David Barrow:

My Mum Always Looks After Me So Much

ISBN 978-0-7112-5195-3

A funny, heartwarming picture book about the love
between a mother and a child.

Little Gorilla is going to the doctor for an injection.
His mum says it's because she has to look after him.
But that's the problem: his mum always looks after
him *so much*. First she makes him eat broccoli,
then whenever he sneezes he has to put on an extra
sweater. And now an injection! But with a sweet
surprise in store, Little Gorilla soon learns that
being looked after isn't *all* bad.